RORY BOYLE

METAL PIECES

for B flat trumpet & piano

THE ASSOCIATED BOARD OF
THE ROYAL SCHOOLS OF MUSIC

METAL PIECES

1

GOOD AS GOLD

RORY BOYLE

AB 2277

METAL PIECES
1
GOOD AS GOLD

TRUMPET in B♭

RORY BOYLE

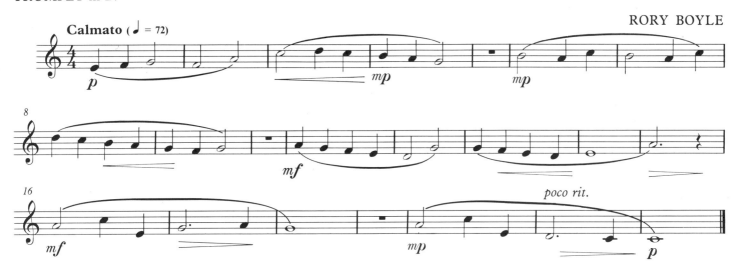

2
NERVES OF STEEL

AB 2277

3
LEAD WEIGHTS

4
IRON FILINGS

5
SILVER LINING

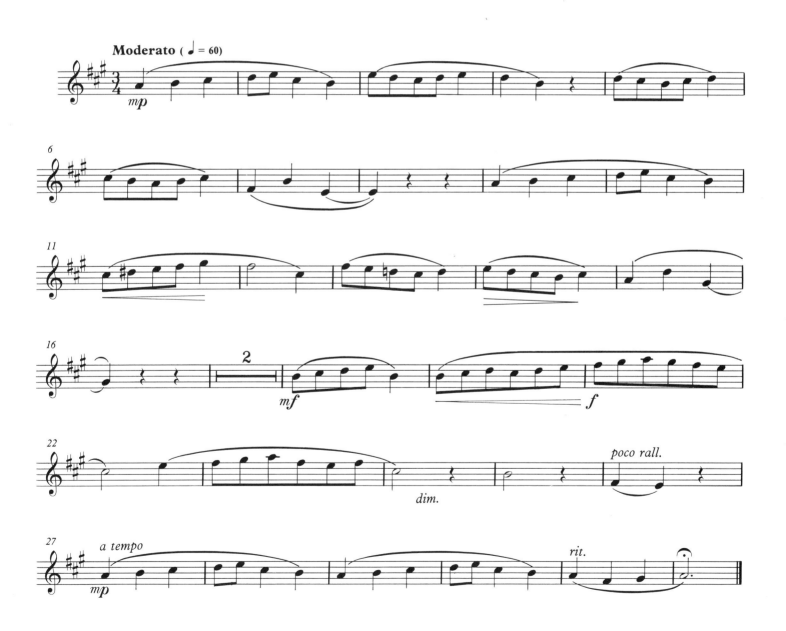

6
BOLD AS BRASS

2
NERVES OF STEEL

3
LEAD WEIGHTS

4
IRON FILINGS

5
SILVER LINING

6
BOLD AS BRASS